MW01517322

CATRINA WHITEHEAD

FALL ON YOUR KNEES

Catrina Whitehead

ISBN:978-1-968792-37-4

CH. 1
ARE WE THERE YET? FIVE MILES FROM BETHLEHEM

By the time Carol headed home from the office, she felt numb. Another late night because peace on earth doesn't translate to work flow at a law office at the end of the year. Rain streamed down the car window. Bright lights blurred through sheets of water forming auras and stars, making the world surreal. More lights than at any time of the year. Everywhere, brightly lit Christmas decorations announced the season.

A sigh escaped, leaving a cloud of visible cold air. Only three weeks until Christmas. The world rejoiced—or at least shopped. Passing the local mall, the parking lot was crammed full. Traffic slowed to a crawl in her lane. Annoyed, she watched the pattern of her windshield wipers blurring and clearing the multi-colored lights.

She turned into her neighborhood. The neighbors had their lights up, but her house was still dark. As she triggered the garage door opener and the car coasted from the downpour into the dry, grey garage space, Carol breathed out slowly. As if on signal, her work shoes felt suddenly unbearable.

Limping from the kitchen to the living room, she chided herself, *You should put them up in the bedroom!* As if the pep talk would work when she was this tired. Her inner child done pretending to adult, she kicked off the pumps the moment they hit carpet. Off went the work blazer, set onto the edge of the couch. *A few more things to put away another day.* She plopped her briefcase beside her recliner, removed her laptop, and collapsed into the cushiony chair.

Looking at her meal plan for the day, the thought of cooking felt like another stone added to the mental backpack she'd been carrying. Wednesday night. No one else home for dinner. Grant was out of town for the week attending a business conference. The twins at a high school event. Presumably gotten fast food on their way after reading her text about working late. Clarissa, now in her first semester of college, was out on a date. Alone in the house, Carol gave herself permission to order in. One less decision. One less thing to do. A large pizza so there would be leftovers in the refrigerator if the rest of them arrived back hungry.

Carol's phone mapped the order's progress. Beeped each time a new step was completed. Order accepted. Payment accepted. Pizza in progress. Delivery picked up. *Beep, beep.* It set her nerves off every time, like a virtual slavedriver forcing her to impulsively check new messages, wondering who had texted or emailed—what new demand. Her cortisol switch never turned off.

She checked the screen once more, watching the driver's progression nearing the house. *Beep.* The screen announced, "Your driver, Juan, is approaching." Carol smiled. The names were a small sense of amusement. This time the Mexican guy delivered Italian food. She watched as the blip moved from the curb to the porch. Waited until the doorbell rang and the blip left. Safe to retrieve her dinner without the assessment of Juan.

As she opened the door, next to the pizza box, another delivery. She mentally noted, *It must be the Christmas devotional I ordered a few days ago. The ad seemed to pop onto my landing page like a gentle nudge—or a calculated algorithm that could sense my seasonal blues.* Carol picked up both boxes and set them in the kitchen.

Two slices of cheesy pizza later, Carol returned to the kitchen to put the leftovers in the refrigerator. Fed but still empty, she stared at the brown box still sitting on the counter. A moment of hesitation. Hope or just another assignment? She grabbed scissors and slit the tape open. The devotional—"Gifts". The shiny cover mocked her.

Her feelings hadn't changed since she ordered it. She stared at the cover.

Lord, I'm not in the mood for Christmas this year. My clients are grinchy. The crowds and traffic are annoying. The family schedule is already packed tight enough. We've already started the yearly heated drama about who is hosting and on what dates. I've been working so many late nights. My house is a disaster. I'm exhausted. But I'm sorry. This season is supposed to be a time of joy and remembering Your birth. Can You help me get my heart in the right place? Can You bring Christmas to me?

No answer.

She opened the book and read:

CHAPTER 1: INTRODUCTION

We're going to take a deep dive into the Christmas story—not in a cozy, sentimental way, but in a way that digs under the layers of familiarity. My hope is twofold:

1. For us to see the Christmas story with fresh eyes, and
2. That you actually feel refreshed in this season instead of wrung out by it or

```
derailed by
expectations   by   the   time
Christmas arrives.
```

```
That   word   refreshed   isn't
fluff. Scripture says we are
refreshed by God's Spirit and
by each other. I'm hoping that
this   time   together   talking
about   Christmas   can   both
ground us in the richness of
God's Word and help us process
the stresses and expectations
of the season, together, being
honest   about   the   cultural
pressures and stress that can
creep   into   our   intentions
around Christmas.
```

Carol paused. Flinched. Maybe God had been listening as she'd been driving through an overly lit but overwhelmingly unilluminated pre-Christmas world tonight. She lifted a prayerful thought. *Lord, refresh my spirit so I can see Christmas through Your eyes.* She read on.

```
JESUS' ARRIVAL WAS EASY TO MISS
```

```
Let's   start   here:   Jesus'
```

7

arrival was almost invisible. It was easy to miss!

Consider the Magi, who we also call Wise Men. They were Gentile scholars, probably from Persia, and started their journey before the nativity even happened. The star didn't lead them to the manger like we often think. The star announced the Christ-child's birth. They had a very long journey. So, by the time they showed up, Jesus was likely two years old. We put the Wise Men in our nativity sets as if they were kneeling next to shepherds, but that's artistic license.

They left everything, traveled perhaps years on foot and camel, just to find a baby. They weren't Jewish. They didn't have the Scriptures. But they were hungry enough to find Jesus to interrupt their entire lives in order to search for Him.

Now contrast them to the Jewish leaders. They lived five miles away in Jerusalem. They'd studied prophecy in the Scriptures their whole lives. When Herod asked where the Messiah would be born, they could quote Micah instantly: "Bethlehem." And yet—they never went. Five miles. Think about that. Men who had studied prophecy their whole lives didn't bother to check if prophecy had actually come true. Their head knowledge never made the five-mile journey to their hearts.

That's the danger of familiarity: head knowledge that never travels the short distance to the heart. We think we know the story, so we stop seeking. And in the process, we can completely miss Him. The Magi crossed deserts. The leaders couldn't cross town.

If the religious leaders missed Jesus, what makes us think we're immune to missing Him now? Here's the uncomfortable parallel: we can decorate, gather, volunteer at church, or even lead services in December—never actually seeking Him ourselves. The culture buries Jesus under Santa and shopping; the church buries Him under the comfortableness of traditions and distractions of busy serving. Both miss the point.

Carol's mind turned to her list of Christmas expectations. She volunteered every Christmas to help decorate the church and greet people for the Christmas Eve service. There was that cookie exchange party her sister hosted every year. She'd already created an Excel spreadsheet of all the dishes she planned to make for their Christmas family dinner, along with a shopping list and cleaning plan—if she could squeeze time away from work. All good. But did the precision planning leave space to seek Jesus?

Carol headed to the kitchen to make a cup of peppermint tea. Taking the steaming cup back to her recliner, she resumed reading.

OUR PRESSURES TODAY

Christmas today? It can be heavy. Family expectations and drama. Financial strain. Hosting. Gift lists. Lonely moments when the season feels like salt in a wound. Performances and rehearsals stacked on top of already full lives. For some, loneliness or grief makes it even heavier. The first gift we'll look at speaks directly into that weight: myrrh, a symbol of suffering and death.

MYRRH - A SYMBOL OF SUFFERING AND DEATH

Myrrh is a resin from a thorny tree. It seeps out like tears from a wound. That's not sentimental imagery—that's brutal foreshadowing. From day one, Jesus was marked for suffering. The very name myrrh means "bitter." Already you hear echoes of the crown of thorns and the Man of Sorrows.

The first Wise Man's gift wasn't random perfume—it was prophetic. Jesus was born to die, and through His death, we are healed.

In the ancient world, myrrh had many uses: perfume, medicine, anointing oil. But its most sobering use was embalming. When John tells us about Jesus' burial, he says Nicodemus and Joseph of Arimathea brought 75 pounds of spices, including liquid myrrh. That's an extraordinary amount—normally reserved for royalty. They soaked linen in it, wrapped His body, and the sticky resin hardened like a cocoon. Days later, the women brought more myrrh to finish the burial process.

Do you see the picture? Jesus wasn't wrapped in a sheet He could shrug off. He was encased. Which makes the resurrection even more staggering. He didn't just "wake up"—He passed through death and grave clothes like a butterfly through its chrysalis or in a burst of miraculous nuclear energy. From the start, even His birthday gifts pointed forward to His sacrificial death and victorious resurrection.

Carol felt the heaviness in her limbs. Her soul cried out, *Oh, Lord, we keep calling it Your birthday, but it was leading to Your death from your first breath! Even your first gift.*

APPLICATION

This year, God isn't asking us to survive Christmas. He's inviting us to be refreshed in Him—to seek Him, worship Him, and carry that refreshment into our volunteer teams, families, and church services, so singing songs, playing instruments, cooking meals, and all our other Christmas activities point not just to the traditional story of Christmas, but points people toward the true gift of Christmas in Christ Himself. So here are the things we need to ponder:

Are we traveling like the Magi or sitting like the scholars?

Are we willing to interrupt our lives, to seek Him intentionally this season? Or are we too close, too familiar, too comfortable—settling for knowing the story without actually encountering the Savior?

Are we seeking Jesus with hunger, or just working around Him because we're too busy or too familiar?

Carol closed the book gently. Was it all so different now? Santa's arrival was certainly hard to miss! But Jesus? The distance between a shopping mall and a nativity manger? The distance between hands volunteering at the church Christmas Eve service and a heart seeking the Christ Child? Why did the arrival of a true Christmas feel so elusive and far away this year?

She walked to the dark window to close the blinds on the night. Rain was still pelting down. Catching her reflection in the glass, Carol caught tired eyes staring back at her. Too tired to seek? *Am I still sitting five miles away?*

Rustling at the front door. Either the twins back from practice or Clarissa returning from her date. Family bustle breaking the silence of the house and her contemplation.

CATRINA WHITEHEAD

CH. 2
THE BEST LAID PLANS REQUIRE MYRRH

Carol woke up to a tickle in her throat. Panic rose. *No! No! NO! I have a major hearing in a week! Deadlines! I don't have time to be sick.*

Struggling to the kitchen, nothing sounded good. Her old friend, coffee, sounded abominable. Carol finally settled on an English Breakfast tea and a piece of toast.

Sneeze! The 16-year-old twins walked in. Marcus made a face. "*Ewww.* Mom, you sick? Gross!"

Carol replied, stuffy and nasal. "Looks like. Clarissa already headed to class. You guys are on your own for breakfast. I don't want to get you sick, too."

The twins exchanged a glance before Michael shouted, "Fast food! I'll drive."

As they bounded toward the garage, leaving the house eerily quiet. Carol's tea was ready. Back at her recliner, computer open, she sipped throat-warming comfort and logged onto her office calendar. A color-coded rainbow filled the screen. She searched for white space representing margin, knowing it barely existed. At least no red for court hearings or deep burgundy for immovable deadlines. But way too many bands of orange meetings that clients could automatically schedule from her website.

At least this is only Saturday. I have time to kick this. If I can. With a history of simple colds turning into deep bronchitis, this requires a strategic response.

Some research on AI fueled by desperation to stay at least partially upright yielded an order of respiratory support supplements, a dozen cans of soup, and every form of hydration in the store.

Lord, I know you only want what's good for me and didn't make me get sick. But did you allow it? Did you let my body call a time-out so my soul could seek?

A decision about the client meetings would need to follow soon, but the devotional book on her side table caught Carol's eye.

Wait a minute, Lord! Wasn't I just reading about myrrh and healing? So why this—now?

A nudge in her spirit made her pick the book back up to keep reading.

CHAPTER 2: THE GIFT OF

MYRRH (CONTINUED)

Last chapter we started unpacking the Wise Men's first gift—myrrh—and saw how it pointed to Jesus' suffering and death. Today, we're going to zoom out and see the bigger picture: where else myrrh shows up in Scripture, and how every reference layers meaning onto who Jesus is for us.

THE WOMEN MYRRH-BEARERS

After Jesus died, Nicodemus and Joseph of Arimathea wrapped His body in strips of linen soaked with about 75 pounds of myrrh and spices. That amount was extraordinary—reserved for kings.

But the story doesn't end there. At dawn after the Sabbath, a group of women came hurrying to the tomb with more myrrh. They weren't content with the hasty burial before sundown. They wanted to honor Jesus with their own hands, at their own expense. These women, sometimes called the Myrrh-Bearers, became the first witnesses of the resurrection. In fact, they were commissioned to carry the good news back to the Apostles. In church history, they're sometimes honored as "equal to the Apostles."

From the beginning, myrrh is tied to the courage and devotion of these devoted women followers who refused to let Jesus' death be the end of His story. Notice the irony: in a culture where women's testimony wasn't considered legally valid, God entrusted the most important announcement in history to women carrying jars of myrrh.

So, in the Gospels, myrrh isn't just about embalming. It's tied to devotion, courage, and the unexpected honor God gives to those the world overlooks.

Carol sat back. *I'm so glad I wasn't a woman*

in those times. Lord, I'm grateful that you saw and honored women even when society and culture didn't. And it seems like it's still up to women to usher in Christmas. I know family expects me to buy the gifts, decorate and house, hang the stockings, and cook the Christmas meal. So maybe Mamas are still the bearers of Your messages.

She looked around the house. Shoes on the floor. Blazer on the back of the couch. Empty mug on the coffee table. Clutter from every member of the family in various corners. No hint of Christmas to come. Only short weeks away.

The picture of her streaming rainbow of demands flashed in her mind. How was she supposed to usher in Christmas? And now sick? She picked up the devotional book again, hesitant. Hadn't it promised to bring refreshment, not more pressure and to-dos?

MYRRH AS PURIFICATION

In Esther 2, young women from across Persia were gathered into the king's harem to prepare for a single night with Xerxes. For six months they were literally bathed in oil of myrrh before they even met the king.

Why? Two reasons.

- First, myrrh's antiseptic and antibiotic properties healed their skin and erased blemishes. It was a literal beauty treatment.
- Second, and more sobering, myrrh was known in the ancient world as a mild abortifacient. This ensured that if a woman entered the king's chamber, there could be no doubt about whose child she carried.

Carol's breath caught. The thought felt cruel and patriarchal—an abuse of power disguised as purity. Her mind flashed to women she knew who'd faced that impossible decision, and to her sister's quiet heartbreak after yet another miscarriage. *Lord, there's pain on every side of that word. You never meant these stories to shame us, only to show how broken the world can be without You.*

She drew in a slow breath. *Even in a book like Esther, where the earthly king's vanity and ego ruled, You were still weaving redemption underneath it all—preparing a different kind of bride for a different kind of King.*

She took paused a moment before she could read on.

> Push that image forward to us: when we come before the King of Kings, we can't be carrying something into the relationship that undermines our purpose. Our hearts can't be carrying the world's affections. Myrrh says: purity matters in the presence of the King.
>
> Now, in the biblical symbolism of Esther, Xerxes is a "type" of king, and Esther as bride points forward to Christ and His Church. Which means this preparation by myrrh whispers something deeper: when we come before the true King, we can't come carrying rival loves or divided loyalty. Our hearts must belong to Him alone.
>
> So, in Esther, myrrh is about purification and preparation to stand before the king. In Jesus, that

```
purification   is   fulfilled—He
lived  sinlessly,  so  He  could
present His Bride, the Church,
pure and without blemish.
```

Carol closed the book hard and threw it on the side table. It slid and landed on the floor. Coughing hard, Carol sucked on a cough drop.

Lord, I certainly don't feel beautiful right now. And what's with the harsh imagery and guilt trips?

It wasn't an audible voice, and it wasn't her internal thoughts. It was just…there. Recognizable. Gentle but firm. Something she'd learned to recognize as the Holy Spirit—the sheep learn to recognize the voice of the shepherd.

Yes, I know, Lord. It's all competing for my attention. But you want to be my One and Only. You're not trying to take anything away from me, but You want it to flow from that center. Instead, it's so easy to come to You packing everything from my world at the forefront of my attention. My affections?

A feeling of affirmation came packed with something that felt like a warm hug of encouragement to her soul.

Yes, I know I can't figure it out on my own with a calendar and a spreadsheet. I need You to make me beautiful. There were so many times in the Bible that people sought You for physical healings and You met them by making them spiritually whole. I need to be bathed in Your presence to heal the things in my life that need fixing more than my congested lungs. (Not that I wouldn't mind those being healed too.)

Carol picked the book off the floor. It wasn't damaged, but she smoothed the cover nevertheless before opening it back up.

MYRRH AND JESUS OUR HIGH PRIEST

Myrrh also points us to Jesus' role as High Priest. Before Jesus, the sacrifices never ended. They had to be repeated over and over. That's why Hebrews Chapter 4 is so powerful. Jesus is our Great High Priest, tempted as we are yet without sin. He offered Himself once for all, and His blood didn't cover sin temporarily—it removed it permanently. And unlike the Levitical priests, He continues even now as our intercessor in heaven.

Here's where myrrh comes in again. At His crucifixion,

```
Roman  soldiers  offered  Jesus
wine mixed with myrrh. This was
a    common    practice—a    crude
painkiller, numbing the agony
of   crucifixion.  Mark  15:23
records  that  Jesus  tasted  it
but  refused  to  drink.  Why?
Because He chose to absorb the
full  suffering  of  the  cross,
with no shortcuts, no numbing.
He bore every drop of pain, so
that  nothing  in  our  own  pain
would be left uncovered.
```

Carol's spirit felt the weight of the words. *Lord, you were willing to surrender everything for me. The least I can do is surrender my calendar to you.*

She opened her computer back up and scrolled forward through the taunting rainbow all the way to Christmas Eve. If she could make it through the deadlines she'd already committed to, she could black out some time to prepare for Christmas with a little more intention.

Carol mentally took inventory of the Christmas decorations in the garage. For many years, when the kids were younger, she'd started planning the Christmas decorations in August. The whole family teased her about it. There had been the year of the under-the-sea tree with handmade embellished shell ornaments and an aqua mermaid-scale tree skirt. A year the tree was inhabited by a flock of hand-blown glass German bird ornaments. The peacock tree with real peacock feathers amongst the branches and chandelier crystals reflecting the blue and green lights.

Carol smiled as she remembered. It felt like a long time ago. A time before her solo practice had become so demanding. Ghosts of Christmas past.

Lord, you know I got rid of all the Santas and snowmen years ago, but this year I want to go all-in just like you went all-in for me at the cross. I want to have a Christmas theme that reflects my heart's intentions.

As she considered the nativity story, she heard the traditional Christmas lyrics in her heart: "Fall on your knees, O hear the angel voices! O night divine, O night when Christ was born!" *That's it. What I need to do. Surrender to the wonder of Christmas. Fall on my knees in worship.*

She opened a new tab on the computer and entered several Christmas-theme searches. An hour later, her cart was filled. Pillows that read "Fall On Your Knees". A cart full of Christmas decorations to reflect themes of nativity and surrender. Carol resolved to fan the small spark of Christmas spirit that was arising despite the scorched earth of this week taking its toll on both body and spirit. It felt like a tiny space was opening in her heart. There was just no room on her calendar.

After entering her credit card information and the Buy-Now button, Carol realized she was exhausted. It was already mid-afternoon and the day felt unsettling in its unproductivity.

This flu, or bronchitis, or whatever, was taking a deeper hold. *Why does it always happen on a weekend when the doctor's office is closed? Thank goodness our insurance provides for on-line care.* She opened yet another tab on the computer to make an appointment. Surprised the screen simply said wait and the doctor can see you within the next fifteen minutes.

As she waited impatiently, Carol looked again at her calendar and assessed the depth of her cough and the haze of her ballon-head. It would be unfair to expose clients to this. But rescheduling people who already waited two weeks for a space on her hectic schedule could prove dicey. Would they just find someone else? Even though people implied that lawyers must be rich, she had a huge overhead and losing a week was one thing, but the prospect of losing future income stream birthed insecurity.

Lord, I need to trust you've got this. I just surrendered my calendar and now my fear is taking it back. Help me to find courage like the Myrrh-Bearer women to trust You to be my pace setter.

She carefully drafted an out-of-office

message for incoming emails: "I'm currently working remote due to illness, but I'm checking my email for urgent matters."

Next, she created a short email explaining she was out sick and didn't want to pass it along. Customizing it to the client appointments waiting over the next week, she gave each client an option to meet by Zoom, reschedule, or try to handle matters by email. As she hit the final send, there was a shuffling noise. The doctor on the other screen. She winced. *I look like some homeless woman with greasy hair, no makeup, and a wrinkled sweat top, but it just reflects how lousy I feel.*

He proved to be young and impatient. Probably overloaded. It felt like he hardly listened. Didn't care about her prior history with respiratory viruses turning into near-hospitalization experiences and taking her out for more than a month. No antibiotics, but he'd call in a couple of prescriptions at the drive-thru pharmacy. Carol bit back a harsh response.

As the doctor disconnected abruptly, Carol sunk further into the recliner in defeat. Her anger at his dismissive attitude replayed in her head, then she reproached herself. *He's probably had a dozen hypochondriacs on the line already today and is navigating a long list of waiting calls. Being bitter isn't going to make me better. All I can do is keep hydrating, resting, and everything else I researched this morning that doesn't require a prescription. I wonder if the script he wrote is really what I need. What do I need?*

The closed devotional book caught her weary eyes. *Maybe there's a different kind of prescription?* As she read the title to the next section, her mouth formed into a wry smile.

MYRRH AS HEALING

Strangely, this resin most associated with death is also associated with healing. In the ancient world, myrrh was used as an antiseptic for wounds, in perfumes, and even in dental treatments. Modern science confirms its potency: studies show it has antibacterial and even shown to kill breast cancer cells.

Which is why Isaiah's words ring so true: "By His stripes we are healed." The very suffering He refused to dull becomes the source of our healing—spiritually from sin, and sometimes physically, according to God's will.

Okay, Lord, I'm doing what I can. When I've reached the end of the things I can control, that's where I can take it to You in its incompleteness. I know You're always with me, even as I'm navigating this challenging week. If it's Your will, help me heal quickly. And lance the anger in my heart like the Great Physician that You are, so the bitterness can seep out and your healing peace can act as a balm.

Carol texted Clarissa: "Prescription called in at the pharmacy drive-thru. Can you pick it up for me on your way home?"

Determining max grossness levels were imminent, Carol forced herself to take a hot shower. It felt good to be clean outside as much as her prayers had been helping wash her clean on the inside, but she emerged exhausted by the small effort.

She withdrew a cozy blanket from the pile of things waiting for a chill in the weather. Carol gathered its minky softness around her. As she closed her eyes, she drifted into a healing sleep.

SUMMARY

The Magi's first gift wasn't just exotic perfume. Myrrh was a prophetic symbol that captured Jesus' identity in layers:

- Purity – the preparation needed to stand before the King, fulfilled in Christ's sinlessness.
- Priesthood – the High Priest who offers not another's blood, but His own, once for all.
- Suffering – the choice to endure agony without numbing, so nothing in our brokenness would be left out.
- Healing – the resin that cleanses wounds pointing to the Savior who heals body and soul.

RESPONSE QUESTIONS

1.	The Myrrh-Bearer women kept showing up, even when hope seemed gone. Where do you feel challenged to show up for Jesus in devotion right now?

2.	Esther's preparation with myrrh suggests we can't carry things of the world into the King's presence. What are some ways our hearts can get "divided"—carrying competing affections—when God calls us to belong to Him fully? What worldly attachments do you feel the Spirit pressing you to release?

3.   Jesus refused the numbing wine. Where do you tend to "numb out" in life instead of facing pain with Him?

4.   Which of myrrh's meanings—purity, priesthood, suffering, or healing—do you most need to lean into this season?

CH. 3
SOUNDS OF SILENCE OR PSYCHOSIS?

Carol woke with a start—2 a.m.? *I must have fallen asleep hard in the recliner? Probably best to sleep upright. I think my fever broke. The kids must have fended for themselves. They've been so quiet and tried not to wake me. I feel like such a bad mom.*

She hit the flashlight function on her phone. Something white on the side table caught her eye. A small white bag with a stapled receipt. A quick inspection confirmed—Clarissa had quietly left the prescriptions. No antibiotics, but two bottles of pills and an inhaler. *Hmmm...*

A sense of dread and panic jolted her wide awake. *It's technically Monday morning. Do I have meetings to get to?*

Fumbling onto email on the phone, there were a raft of client messages. She took a deep breath before opening them one by one. A few notes of true sympathy, one terse inquiry if she was up to task while sick, and others that feigned understanding but read flat. Clearly clients, not friends. Their legal solutions app was down for maintenance at an inconvenient time, and they just wanted to know when it would be fully online again. No one wanted to share air space—a relief.

Sleep having completely fled, Carol triaged the responses to realign her calendar—rearranging current work and ensuring no additional appointments would be scheduled until there was adequate time to complete it. That completed, she finally shut the computer—4 a.m. *Thank goodness the kids are old enough to fend for themselves. I have to get some rest.*

When she woke again, the house was empty and quiet once more.

Three document review assignments and a post-arbitration remote meeting with a judge in the early afternoon. But nothing that wouldn't wait until lunch.

I'm feeling better, but I can tell that I won't get completely well or might relapse if I try to keep a normal schedule this week. Thank you, Jesus, for helping me find a way to make it manageable.

After a quick bowl of soup, Carol forced herself to concentrate, summoning the inner professional to get comments back to one client on escrow instructions for a complicated commercial sale, drafting a contract for another client who had been recently sued and realized there were holes in their client agreements, and answered a demand letter from an attorney threatening to sue another client if his own client didn't get his way.

There was just enough time to grab a quick cup of tea before cleaning up in preparation for the remote meeting with the judge. Carol cringed at the thought it included video. It wouldn't do to just show her picture instead of allowing the video camera. As she applied the peach shade of blush that made her look least sallow. She considered, *I'm not sure how much talking my voice will take today. And I'm not sure if I want the judge to know I'm sick or if I just want to fake my way through this call.* Her hair was clean, but the curling iron would only remedy so much. Thank goodness the virtual meeting meant a small screen, hopefully not allowing too much detail. She swiped on a bright shade of lipstick and called it good enough.

Thankfully, the judge only had a few questions. Ordered a final closing brief. Opposing counsel's comments were brief. Carol smiled and kept her personal problems to herself thanks to a blast from the inhaler in advance. She'd passed for healthy, but it cost her more than the cough.

You're pushing again. In a way that could bite back. If you want the Christmas that's been unfolding in your heart, you'd better dial back.

She looked again at the mocking calendar. It was goading her—keeping her cortisol levels swirling—but her brain told her there was nothing that would explode before tomorrow. She forced herself to tune into a romance channel running a Christmas movie marathon. Dozed off about halfway through the movie about a New York lawyer who gave it all up to save and run Grampa's apple farm and find her dream man.

A short time later, her senses came back online. Television still on. Her half-awake brain tried to make sense of the discrepancies, then realized, another movie in the Seasonal Showcase. Same actors. Different but comically similar plot. Chicago advertising executive spends Christmas at Auntie's failing B&B, leaves her job to take it over, and it makes enormous amounts of money while never seeming to have more than a few guests, need cleaning, or require more than baking apple pies. Comes complete with county man who works at his parent's hardware store but isn't broke.

Carol started to chuckle, realizing she'd been caught up in the holiday haze created by the ubiquitous channel. Then the chuckle turned into a cough. She grabbed for another cough drop. As she did, her eyes landed on the devotional. *Might as well put something more meaningful into my head.* She opened to the next chapter.

CHAPTER 3: WISE MAN WITH GIFT OF FRANKINCENSE

WHAT IS FRANKINCENSE?

Picture one of the Magi kneeling before Jesus. He opens a small chest, and a sharp, pine-like fragrance fills the room. The gift is frankincense, a gum resin from a tree that somehow finds a way to grow in harsh places—even out of bare rock. Its fragrance is reminiscent of Christmas pine, but in the ancient world it carried deeper meaning: worship in the presence of royalty.

Frankincense symbolized kingship. It pointed to Jesus as the King of Kings. In Song of Solomon 1:3, the reference to this spice alludes to the very name of God Himself. From the start, this gift declared that the Child in Bethlehem was no ordinary baby, but Heaven's true King.

FRANKINCENSE IN THE TABERNACLE

Frankincense is often burned as incense. Imagine

stepping inside the ancient tabernacle. Before you stands a golden altar with horns at each corner. Twice each day, morning and evening, Aaron the priest kindled incense there. Exodus 30:7-8 records, "Aaron must burn fragrant incense on the altar every morning when he tends the lamps… and again at twilight so incense will burn regularly before the LORD for the generations to come."

The smoke rising from this altar was a sign of worship and atonement. Just as frankincense was essential in the tabernacle, Jesus is essential to worship today. Without Him, there is no access to God. Through Him, the way is open.

Carol imagined the scented smoke filling the Old Testament tabernacle. Rising to heaven. A constant acknowledgment of the Heavenly King. Worthy of worship. Then the New Testament Jesus. Making a way to access that Heavenly King.

Her eyes closed for a moment, trying to

imagine the perfumed air, then she read on.

FRANKINCENSE AS A SYMBOL OF PRAYER

Incense in Scripture often represents prayer. Revelation 8:4 says, "The smoke of the incense, together with the prayers of God's people, went up before God from the angel's hand."

Let's consider three qualities of frankincense and what they teach us about prayer:

First: It grows out of rock. The frankincense tree thrives in harsh, rocky terrain. Likewise, our prayers must persist even in hard seasons.

Second: It was costly. Frankincense was likely more valuable than gold in the Magi's gifts. True prayer costs us something too—time, focus, humility. It is a sacrifice of praise.

Third: It's pleasing. The

aroma was sweet and delightful. So are prayers that rise from humble, grateful hearts—full of worship, confession, and trust.

But just as when you want to bring your request to an earthly king, you have to get close enough for him to hear. If we want our Heavenly King to hear our prayers, we first need to draw close.

Psalm 100:4 reminds us to "Enter his gates with thanksgiving and his courts with praise." In ancient times, no one saw the king without passing through layers of gates and courtyards. You might shout your requests from the courtyard, but it was most likely to be heard only if you could get an actual audience with the King. Similarly, the ancient tabernacle had outer courts of the Gentiles, then the court of the Jews, and then inner courtyards and then finally the Holy of Holies where God's presence dwelled. Even the priests were extremely limited from access to the Holy of Holies. The people could shout their requests from the courtyards, but it was only when Jesus' died on the cross that the heavy curtain separating the Holy of Holies was torn from top to bottom, symbolizing access to God's presence for everyone through Jesus' sacrifice.

But going back to Psalms, look again at the access symbols. We enter the gates – the far entrance to the holy city – by having thankfulness in our hearts. We get to the courtyard – closer to the King – through praise. It's after we have our hearts in the right place that our prayers have the closest access to God's ears.

The sound of the front door opening broke Carol's thoughts. Next, the hum of a garage door opening. The kids all arrived home within minutes of one another and headed straight to their rooms. Carol closed the book and her eyes.

Lord, my recent prayers have all been driven by the urgency of my needs. Well, perceived urgency at least. I've wanted help with my business, quick recovery from this illness, even safety for my twins with their new driver's licenses. All good, but I sort of barged into the throne room, didn't I? Demanding things from the king? Have I been rude to You when You're so good to me? And it's not just about trying to get close to get what I want. It really is about access. A privilege to be close to the king. I really need to remember that. Can You help me remember? So, I'm thankful for all the good things in my life. I can praise You, not just for being willing to sacrifice everything just to allow me to have access toYyou, but for always wanting the best for me and being patient with me. When I think about those things first, it really puts some perspective into what I want to whisper closely in your ear.

As she replaced the book on the side table thoughtfully, heart full, she turned on her old playlist of Christmas music from last year—a mix of traditional and new releases that all spoke of the truth of the holiday. Still not feeling completely well, Carol headed off the mother guilt by placing a delivery order for Chinese food. A family favorite. She texted the kids. All the way to their bedrooms.

But yelling down the hallway didn't seem to be the way in a modern family.

Waiting for the order to arrive, body still glued to her sick-season recliner, Carol closed her eyes, listening intently to the music. It felt like peace descending into the living room. She smiled as the words to "O Holy Night" lifted quietly to the top of the high ceiling like a prayer. "Fall on your knees. Oh hear the angel voices…"

The doorbell announcing the delivery arrival jarred her back.

Clarissa waltzed into the room and pulled a face. "Oh, God, you're starting with the Christmas music already? I just read a study that Christmas music can make you psychotic." She purposed a dramatic eye roll. "Repetition drives people to insanity."

Michael emerged with a big grin. "Nah, just stressed and depressed."

PRAYER CHALLENGE

This week, ask yourself: What kind of prayers does God delight to answer?

First, He wants authentic prayer. Not rehearsed words, not polished speeches—real conversation.

Second, He wants balanced prayer. Too often our prayers are just lists of requests—what I call "bubble gum prayers," as if God were a vending machine: insert request, receive answer. Instead, prayer is a privilege. It's our chance to invite Him into our decisions, to thank Him, to praise Him, and yes, to bring our needs.

If someone overheard your prayers this week, would they hear a shopping list—or a conversation with your King?

So, before you rush into requests, pause. Enter with thanksgiving. Continue with praise. Then bring your heart to the King who has already given you access. That is the true fragrance of Christmas.

RESPONSE QUESTIONS:

1. Frankincense trees grow out of rock in harsh environments. When have your prayers "grown out of rock"—persisting in a hard or dry season?

2. Frankincense was more costly than

gold. What would it look like for your prayer life to "cost" you something this week (time, comfort, pride, distraction)?

3.   Psalm 100:4 says we enter with thanksgiving and praise. How might shifting the order of your prayers (starting with thanks and praise before requests) change your relationship with God this week?

4.   If someone overheard your prayers, would they hear a shopping list—or a conversation with your King? What one change could help your prayers sound more like conversation than requests?

CH. 4
SILVER TINSEL, POODLES PUPPIES, AND GHOSTS OF CHRISTMAS PAST

Tuesday arrived with the kids humming to their usual routine and Carol beginning to wonder if she'd actually become part of the recliner. Not going to the office didn't mean not working. Solo lawyer translates to never on vacation and never sick. Carol glanced at her schedule. I was still showing old meetings that had been rescheduled. *I could just leave them as placeholders and work on those cases at the times I would have met with the clients.*

It was all beginning to feel manageable. With careful management, Carol's cough seemed like it was at least holding its own, not getting deeper.

There was a commotion on the porch. The sound of a male voice talking on a mobile phone. Shuffling and a muffled bang, then footsteps walking away. Carol peeked out the windows next to the front door. Three packages. *The decorations I ordered on overnight delivery!*

Not willing to wait, Carol dragged them inside and ripped the first box open. The "Fall On Your Knees" pillow shams. An easy first step, Carol replaced the old shams on the couch with her theme covers.

Next, she withdrew a shiny gold camel. Holding it up, a flood of childhood memories played like a movie in her brain. Mom, painstakingly decorating the Christmas tree with thousands of strands of shiny silver tinsel, each individually placed. A well-worn nativity with three plastic camels, silver paint slightly tarnished, each saddle a different color. Kindergarten Carol sitting in a child-size rocking chair, wearing brand-new Christmas Eve pajamas, holding a tiny toy poodle with a satin bow in its fur just above the ear.

She smiled as she gently unwrapped two more camels from the box and placed them carefully on the mantle. *I only hope my own children will look back with nostalgia. Christmas carols and all.*

Placing a few more decorations around the house, Carol realized she couldn't drag the artificial Christmas tree in from the garage without help. It would have to wait until the boys were home from class. As she surveyed the unfinished work, she realized she couldn't procrastinate from work much longer. *Well, maybe just one chapter longer?* She put her Christmas playlist on quietly in the background and searched for the devotional book.

CHAPTER 4: WISE MAN WITH THE GIFT OF GOLD – REFINING & PURITY

SYMBOLISM OF GOLD

The Magi's final gift was gold. At first, gold might seem like an obvious symbol of royalty, but that role was more fittingly represented by frankincense. Jesus never came to wear an earthly crown of gold. Others say gold simply represents Jesus' value—but that's too shallow. Still others point to gold in the tabernacle or to Jesus' everlasting throne—but we've already touched those themes.

So, what does gold symbolize? Let's look at it as a picture of provision, comparison, and refinement.

Carol's face formed a smirk as if she'd just gotten the joke. *Lord, I'm beginning to think there's a lot of Your orchestration in this week. Gold, huh?*

GOLD AS GOD'S PROVISION

Gold was provision to Mary and Joseph. After the Magi's visit, King Herod ordered the massacre of all boys two years old and under in Bethlehem. It was Satan's attempt to snuff out God's plan. Yet God always makes a way. Joseph was warned in a dream to flee to Egypt. How could a poor carpenter suddenly afford such a journey? The gold. God had already provided. So, the first symbolism of gold is this: God equips His people with what they need for His plan to succeed.

Lord, this sickness meant to take me down is being used to build me up. Is that how it works? And the clients that I didn't lose when I had to reschedule? Is that Your provision also? What other ways have you provided for me in the past that I didn't even recognize. What plans are You equipping me for? She read on.

GOLD AS A COMPARISON OF VALUE

In Scripture, gold rarely represents value itself. Instead, it's the standard of comparison. Wisdom is said to be worth more than the purest gold. God's commandments are "better than gold, yes, than fine gold" (Psalm 19:10).

Earthly riches may glitter, but compared to the wealth of God's wisdom, they are nothing. The second takeaway relating to gold is this: God's treasures always outweigh earthly wealth.

Carol felt a twinge of conviction. Gold was also about money. Work had been keeping her busy recently. But the office budget reflected a punishing amount of overhead even before the first funds could pay home bills. Grant contributed too, but her paycheck was critical to the family's finances.

How much is enough, Lord? I have responsibilities and bills to pay. Am I really seeking glitter or just survival? Too busy? Too busy for Your plans, God?

As that small—more felt than heard—voice niggled, Carol looked around the room at her recent purchases.

But, Lord, I bought these things to honor You. Are you really giving me a guilt trip about that now, right as I thought we'd made progress about Christmas priorities?

Carol started to put the book down, but her reading time felt as unfinished as the decorations around her.

```
GOLD AS PURITY AND TESTING
        In Hebrew, the word for
gold is often clarified as
"zahabh"—pure, refined, the
finest.      Gold      throughout
Scripture becomes a symbol of
testing and refining. Our
faith, like gold, is proven
genuine   only   when   passed
through  fire.  At  the  final
judgment,   works   built   on
Christ will remain; impurities
will   be   burned   away.   Our
takeaway: God takes our value
and refines it into something
greater              through
transformation.
```

Carol considered the imagery. *All the things I've worked for here on earth are destined to have their value burned up in the end. They serve a purpose now, but those purposes aren't eternal. Oh Lord, my brain is valuable to my clients, but nothing compared to your wisdom. I know you want to take my faith and make it into something more. Transformation. At my age, it seems like it's been slow, and time is gradually running out. I mean, I try to continually improve myself, but humans are pretty unsuccessful with meaningful change. We get stuck in our processing ruts. You're the Master at creating new things in the human heart.*

That was a heavy thought and there were deadlines to hurdle. Carol put the book reverently aside and turned to client demands for the rest of the afternoon.

With Grant gone, the kids seemed to find things to do with friends in the evenings. *Maybe avoiding my virus?* Marcus and Michael had been home long enough for Carol to nag them into retrieving the huge, dusty Christmas tree box and lugging it to the living room. It sat there, unopened, a reminder that the house was not ready for Christmas. Countdown clicking.

Carol groaned in her head. *Getting all the Christmas stuff out so late means it's only up such a short while, then I have to face all the work of putting it back up again. Nothing in me wants to do this Christmas, Lord. You already can see my heart, so it's no use pretending with You. But you can also see I want to do it anyway as a sacrificial gift. To my family. To my church. Mostly, to You. Help me handle it all with grace! Are there more answers in my Christmas book?*

She looked around. Getting the house in order was important, but it seemed more important to get priorities in order. She opened the cover to read.

GOLD IN THE LETTERS TO THE CHURCHES

The Book of Revelation deepens this picture through two churches with very different lessons.

Sardis: The Church at Sardis was wealthy because of nearby gold deposits. Its king, Croesus, was the first to mint pure gold coins. But the church in Sardis had become spiritually lazy. Jesus warned them to wake up—or He would come like a thief in the night. Sardis reminds us: we can safeguard possessions and yet lose what truly matters by failing to guard our hearts.

Laodicea: The Church at Laodicea prided itself on its banks, minted coins, and self-sufficiency. When an earthquake devastated the city in A.D. 60, Rome offered help, but Laodicea proudly refused: "We did it ourselves." Even their coins proclaimed independence. But in Revelation 3:18, Jesus counseled them: "Buy from me gold refined in the fire, so you can become rich." The Spirit called them "poor, blind, and naked."

Why? Because their faith was counterfeit. They appeared rich but lacked true spiritual value. They needed faith refined by God, not coins stamped by men.

Paul had written to them decades earlier, reminding them that the true riches are "Christ in you, the hope of glory" (Colossians 1:27). All treasures of wisdom and knowledge are hidden in Him.

Carol looked at the gold camels on the fireplace. *We really have made Christmas all about false gold, haven't we? Tinsel, garland, shining lights. And we've done it ourselves. Put our own stamp on it and made a holiday. Not what it was ever meant to be. Crafted of what we get, what we do, and how much we spend. Excess but empty. Lord, I've been trying to do a lot of things myself. Help me start to see things the way You see them instead of how I think they should be.*

She read on.

BEING WEIGHED AND FOUND WANTING

This warning echoes back to Daniel 5. King Belshazzar used sacred gold vessels from God's temple to toast idols of gold and silver. A hand appeared and wrote on the wall: "MENE, MENE, TEKEL, PARSIN." Daniel explained: TEKEL means "you have been weighed on the scales and found wanting." Belshazzar's self-evaluation was five gold stars, but God thought he was worth very little.

REFINED BY FIRE

To be "refined by fire" is to let God strip away what is

false and strengthen what is true. Trials allowed by God are not traps to make us fail but tests to make us pure.

The gold given to Jesus symbolized His own unblemished purity. His worth was tested in the wilderness, in Gethsemane, and at the cross. Only a flawless sacrifice could redeem us. He remained pure, so His death held value. He did it to make us pure too.

Getting a bit tired of the recliner and sameness, Carol set the book aside. She compulsively checked email and then logged onto social media, hoping for a moment of comic relief in the reels to offset the heaviness of the devotional lesson. As she scrolled, a video about refining silver.

Lord, this doesn't seem coincidental. What are you trying to tell me? She hit play.

A man sitting in front of a red-hot furnace, silver article in hand. He began to talk about the ancient process of refining silver in fire. First by heating the silver until the impurities rise to the surface so they could be removed. But cautioning that the silver must always be watched carefully so it isn't damaged by leaving it in the fire too long. And the process was complete when the refiner's image was clearly reflected in the silver.

Carol paused scrolling. *So, I think You're telling me that You let challenges come into my life to purify me but You're always there, watching and making sure it's for a good result and not to hurt me. My transformation won't be complete until I shine back a heart that reflects the image of Christ.*

It was getting late, and Carol's eyes were beginning to get heavy, but the video was like a prod to finish the chapter in the devotional. She glanced to the next page. Just a short paragraph.

VALUING GOD ABOVE ALL ELSE

Gold ultimately asks us: what do we treasure most? Earthly wealth or eternal wisdom? Self- sufficiency or Christ in us? A glittering façade—or faith refined in fire?

The Magi's gift of gold whispered of Jesus' mission: the priceless, pure sacrifice who would restore relationship between God and man.

As Carol closed the book, she closed her

eyes. Dreams followed—of poodle puppies, tinsel trees, and all the things that made past Christmases remain in her heart.

PRAYER CHALLENGE

This week, ask God to refine your heart. Pray that He would reveal any areas where you're relying on your own wealth, effort, or sufficiency instead of on Him. Invite Him to burn away impurities and strengthen what is genuine.

When you face pressures or testing, pause and ask: "Lord, how are you refining me through this? What do You want to purify in me?"

RESPONSE QUESTIONS

1.   The gold given to Jesus provided for His family's escape to Egypt. When has God provided for you in an unexpected way?

2.   Scripture says wisdom and God's commands are worth more than gold. What earthly treasure or comfort do you sometimes value above God's wisdom?

3.   Sardis became spiritually lazy while surrounded by wealth. Belshazzar was "weighed and found wanting." What areas of your life are most vulnerable to "spiritual laziness" when things are going well? If God were to weigh your heart today, what would He find pure— and what might need refining?

4.   Laodicea prided itself on self-

sufficiency, even rejecting outside help. Where in your own life are you tempted to say, "I can do it myself," instead of depending on God?

CH 5
TEAR BOTTLES

Carol woke in the middle of the night. Another night in the recliner to keep the cough recovery on track resulted in a kinked neck. Thirsty, she glanced around the room—just enough porch light shining from the front door windows to navigate. Or so she thought until she tripped on the Christmas tree box and went sailing forward, knees connecting hard with carpet with an *oomph*.

Gathering herself, she was grateful it was just an ego bruise. As she put her hands on the couch to help steady a rise back to her feet, the dim light caught two pillows: *Fall On Your Knees.*

She shook her head. *Sometimes, Lord, you have a really strange sense of humor about what you allow in my life. But if that's what it takes to humble me onto my knees, I'm not going to argue.*

* * * * *

The next several days of her forced office quarantine rolled past in a blur of deadlines and mundane family life. When Friday arrived, she exhaled—a light day, maybe time to assemble that Christmas tree.

The phone rang. Her sister's caller ID. She pushed connect.

"Hi, Sissy. What's going on in your corner of the world?"

"Hey, Stinky. We haven't planned Christmas yet."

Carol drew a steadying breath. *Straight to the point, complete with childhood nicknames.* Bracing. "What did you have in mind?"

"Well, Mom's taking Christmas Eve this year. I assume you'll want Christmas morning just for your little crew. We're doing Christmas Day open-house style. And my annual Christmas Cookie Exchange is next week. Did you get the invite in the mail? I didn't get your RSVP yet."

Groan. The Christmas Cookie Exchange. She loathed it, but attendance? Inescapable. Ditching a full-on sister betrayal. First, the chore of baking five dozen cookies to take to the exchange. Like rainbow calendar had a spot for that nonsense! Then, a group of her sister's model-thin friends exclaiming over the parade of every cookie from the Christmas Cookie Encyclopedia—never eating one. A huge assortment boxed for each to take home. Once there, Carol's best defense? Plan vegetarian dinner and hope the twins would ravage the sugar fest.

Silence on the phone line demanded an answer. "Of course! On my calendar. Did I forget to let you know?" Forcing a cheery tone, Carol was glad her sister couldn't see her face.

"Oh good. You know, you're too busy. We don't see each other often enough. And Mom—she won't always be around."

"I know. It will be great to see everyone. Deadlines calling—see you next week."

Escaped complete, before being forced to decline the open house overload and cause a kerfuffle. Carol added the dreaded Cookie Exchange on her schedule in turquoise blue—personal appointments. Scanning for a cookbook with decent cookie recipes, her eyes were drawn back to the devotional. Moving around was making her cough again anyway. She sat down to calm her soul and read.

CHAPTER 5:- WISE MAN WITH THE GIFT OF GOLD – FRIENDSHIP
GOLD AS A SYMBOL OF RELATIONSHIP

Gold doesn't just symbolize provision or purity. In the story of the Magi, it also reflects relationship. The wise men acted as true friends to the Holy Family—

giving them gold to fund their flight to Egypt and refusing to betray them to Herod.

This week, we'll look at gold as a picture of friendship, mentoring, and discipleship. Sometimes we think of these as "special" roles, but Scripture shows they are woven into everyday life. At its simplest, we mentor whenever we influence others. Proverbs 27:17 puts it this way: "As iron sharpens iron, so one person sharpens another."

When believers walk together—sharing, encouraging, even correcting—we're shaping each other. Those further along in the faith are called to guide those still growing. When one of us is hurting, others help bear the burdens. That's part of God's design for His people: we need each other.

Do I need other people? Most of my friends have been soccer season moms—pleasant enough while the kids were on the same team, then done. That one neighbor that exchanged kid picks ups with me—magical until she moved only a year later. Family? Family can be so complicated!

Her eyes caught on "influence", her heart picturing her children.

Lord, Clarissa just told us she wants to transfer to a different college. Away next year. Please bring friends around her that are good influences. Same with the boys—especially the boys. And I guess we're all meant to pay that prayer forward, so show me where I need to be a good influence.

That thought in mind, she read on.

CHARACTERISTICS OF GOOD FRIENDS

1. Encouragement. We're commanded to build each other up. Encouragement means giving courage, speaking life, lending strength. True friends fan faith into flame.

2. Confidentiality. Trust is the bedrock of friendship. Proverbs 20:6 says many claim to be faithful, but few truly are. Proverbs 16:28 warns that gossip destroys

friendships.

Gossip, literally "tale-bearing," means carrying around stories that are not ours to tell. Sharing praise directly with someone is encouragement. Sharing their private struggles with others—that's gossip.

Sometimes gossip disguises itself as a prayer request: "Please pray for so-and-so because…" But Jesus calls us to take every thought captive (2 Corinthians 10:5), which means also taking every word captive. Our speech should be filtered through Him.

At its root, gossip is self-serving. It makes us feel important, superior, or "in the know." It's conversation that lacks proper boundaries. It can happen when we aren't properly engaging our filters or considering our words. One of my favorite Bible verses says we should take every thought captive to Christ! Specifically, 2 Corinthians 10:5 advises us, "We demolish arguments and every pretension that sets itself up against the knowledge of God, and we take captive every thought to make it obedient to Christ." Jesus should always be our filter as we are engaging in communication.

True friendship does the opposite: it seeks the good of the other, even when that means keeping silent.

BRINGING IT TOGETHER

The Magi's gold symbolized relationship through provision, loyalty, and sacrifice. God wants us to value our earthly relationships too—especially when they encourage, protect, and lift one another in times of grief. He honors the ways we love and support one another.

That phrase, Lord. One of my favorites in the Bible. "Take every thought captive to make it obedient to Christ." As a lawyer, I keep confidences professionally, but how well do I capture thoughts?

An image rose: a field of flashing, jewel-blue butterflies. Chasing them with a big net. Then the image turned ugly. Some of the butterflies became ugly, with huge stingers. Her memory echoed curses. Hardened clients hurling creative iterations and combinations of swear words. If she heard enough, one might slip out when she got cut off in traffic. Then came echoes of past words that had slashed deep leaving scars.

Lord, help me keep my Jesus filter in place. I might not be able to stop the thoughts, but I can hand them to You before they sting someone else.

* * * * * *

As dusk began to overtake the day, Carol's phone rang—her best friend, Liz. The voice on the line strained.

Alarms bells. Carol took the phone to a quiet room as she spoke. "What's wrong?"

"You know me. I just needed someone to talk to. It's Rebecca. Miscarried. A baby boy. They'd only just told us a few days before. A pre-Christmas surprise and now he's gone."

Carol froze, processed. Far enough along to know sex. "I'm so sorry, Liz. He would have been your first grandbaby. How are they?"

"Devastated of course. And I don't know what to say to them. So many people treat a miscarriage like it was a baby that never happened. Most of their friends didn't even know she was pregnant. It's hard to know who she can grieve with."

Carol paused a moment. "I wish phones could send hugs." It was hard to know what else to say. She softly added, "Jesus knows and cares. And he gives friends to us to help encourage us and bear our burdens. We can talk more about it as much or as little as you like."

Carol could hear Liz's husband murmuring in the background. "Greg wants us to go to the hospital to see her. They're releasing her in the morning, but I needed a friend tonight."

As they hung up, Carol's eyes welled with tears imaging if it were Clarissa in Rebecca's place.

Lord, why do You allow such sorrow right before Christmas?

As the lament rose, Carol remembered how the Christmas devotional paralleled so many other things in her life recently. Coincidence or providence? She decided to put it to the test and turned another page.

TEAR BOTTLES

Scripture gives us a striking image in Psalm 56:8: "You have kept count of my tossings; put my tears in your bottle." God doesn't just notice our sorrow—He treasures it.

The image of a tear bottle wasn't only poetic. In Roman times, women literally collected tears in glass bottles and left them at tombs as a sign of mourning. In the Victorian era, special bottles had vented caps so collected tears could evaporate; when they dried up, mourning was declared over. Even during the American Civil War, some women saved tears until their husbands returned—or, if they never did, sprinkled them over the grave. Imagine that: jars of tears offered as memorials of love.

Now imagine this: God Himself keeping your tears. Not one unnoticed. Not one wasted. One day, in heaven, perhaps we will pour out those bottles at His feet—declaring that every sorrow was worth it in light of His victory. And one day, the bottles won't be

needed at all. Revelation 21:4
promises: "He will wipe every
tear from their eyes. There
will be no more death or
mourning or crying or pain."

Until then, God keeps
count. He remembers. He weeps
with us. The Bible even tells
us He draws especially close to
us when we're brokenhearted.

What a beautiful image Lord. Carol
remembered some of the tears she'd shed over the
years. Imagined them stored in a brilliant cut-crystal
bottle, carefully inventoried by a loving Savior. Not
wasted. Counted as God weeps with us. *I can't wait
to pour them out at your feet, Jesus. And thank you
for the perfect thing to share with Liz. I know she's
filling her tear bottle tonight, but one day you'll
restore everything to what You intended in the
beginning. No more sorrows. No more tears.*

PRAYER CHALLENGE

This week, bring your friendships and your sorrows before God. Ask Him to show you how to be an encourager, a confidant, and a safe place for others.

As you pray, remember Psalm 56:8 — every tear you have shed is known, counted, and treasured by God. Picture Him holding your tear bottle, not as a reminder of endless sorrow, but as a promise that one day He will wipe every tear from your eyes.

Pray also for your friends who may be carrying silent grief. Ask God to help you notice, listen, and walk with them so they know they are not alone.

RESPONSE QUESTIONS

1. Proverbs 27:17 says "iron sharpens iron." Who has God placed in your life to sharpen you? Who might you be called to mentor, encourage, or guide?

2. Psalm 56:8 says God keeps your tears in His bottle. What is a sorrow you're carrying even in a season that's supposed to be full of joy? How does it change your perspective to know that God values even the tears you wish had never fallen?

3. Gossip breaks trust, but encouragement builds it. Think about your recent

conversations: are they more often carrying stories that aren't yours—or carrying courage to someone who needs it?

    4.   Revelation 21:4 promises that one day God Himself will wipe away every tear. Grief has an expiration date in heaven. How does that promise shape the way you endure sorrow now? Have you ever thought of your bottle of stored tears as a beautiful gift you will someday be able to empty at Jesus' feet?

CATRINA WHITEHEAD

CH 6
THE KING'S CHRISTMAS LIST

Rolling into the weekend, Carol felt well enough to resume her volunteer duties at the church and ease back into a full work schedule. Just a couple Sundays before Christmas, the church was filled with majestically tall, decorated Christmas trees and the sounds of traditional carols as well as some of the latest Christmas worship selections. Carol wasn't feeling well enough yet to stand at the door as a greeter, so she switched places with one of the ladies manning the ticket table for the Women's Christmas Tea.

Next week, she hoped to be back on the music team—if her voice allowed. For now, being away from the recliner was refreshing.

When she got home from church, Carol was tired in a good way. Grant was arriving home tonight. She decided to enjoy one more day of not cooking. She called down the hallway. "Whoever wants

Mexican food, come give me your delivery order."

A short bit of wrangling later, dinner ordered, Carol was ready to reclaim the recliner again. That, and start decorating the Christmas tree. As she struggled the pieces from the box. Michael peeked in. "Hey, Mom, let me give you a hand with that."

She smiled, but he vanished down the hall before she could thank him, the smile melting into confusion. His voice echoed. "Hey, Lazy Butt, get in here and help Mom with the tree."

Both boys returned and made a show of putting together the three sections of the artificial tree. Carol held her breath as they plugged in the lights. Victory. All good since last year. She grabbed a box of ornaments and looked expectantly at the boys. "Should I make us some hot cocoa while we decorate?"

Marcus spoke for them. "Not our thing, Mom. We got the manly work done. All yours now." With that they headed back to their private domains.

Carol spent the next two hours hanging Christmas ornaments, "psychosis-inducing" Christmas music playing softly in the background. She looked at the tree approvingly, then took the final ornament from its box—a Christmas pickle. New this year, she'd read there was a tradition where the person who finds the green glass oddity gets a small gift. She smiled as she hung it deep toward the trunk of the tree where it should be hard to spot. She'd announce the game when the whole family was back together.

The dusty box was the only thing out of place. Grant's plane would land soon. She called down the hall for the boys to help her put the empty container back in the garage. Marcus entered the living room, glanced at the tree, and announced, "What's with the glass pickle?"

Carol groaned. Two seconds. Done.

Box gone. Game defeated. Carol returned to the devotional to try to replenish some holiday cheer the pickle had soured.

CHAPTER 6 - KING & GOD & SACRIFICE + THE STAR

Now we turn to the star of the nativity. Its meaning is threefold: Guide, Light, and Passed Torch.

STAR AS SPIRITUAL LIGHT: BORN INTO A DARK WORLD

Galatians 4:4 says, "When the set time had fully come, God sent his Son." Jesus was born at a perfectly chosen moment — into a time in history of particular darkness—a world steeped in law, Roman rule, and a dimness of spiritual enlightenment.

The law had served as a guardian, showing God's people that they could never meet His standards alone. Its weight was designed to break human pride and reveal the need for a Savior. At that "full" moment, Jesus came to redeem and adopt us as God's children.

Into that darkness, the Light was born.

Looking at the lights of the newly decorated Christmas tree warming the living room, Carol reflected.

The law. A guardian. It certainly wasn't a solution then. Isn't today either. Court is about giving away the decision about who's right and wrong to a judge. Solves the "thing" of the dispute, but it often leaves relationships shattered. No wonder there's a tremendous dissatisfaction rate even when people win in a courtroom. God's laws are no different. Contracts we would never be able to uphold. A strict judge. No relationship in it. Only darkness. It only reveals that we need Jesus to save us from that fate. Where mercy meets judgment.

STAR AS GUIDE: FREED TO

PURSUE SPIRITUAL MATURITY

But freedom from sin is just the beginning. Jesus didn't free us so we could stand still — He freed us so we could grow. That's the process we call transformation—becoming more like Jesus. Free to become spiritually mature with the Great Counselor, the Holy Spirit.

Paul counsels in Galatians 5 not to indulge the flesh but to walk by the Spirit, bearing the fruit of that Spirit — love, joy, peace, patience, kindness, goodness, faithfulness, gentleness, self-control. Letting the Spirit become our guide. Romans 8:1-5 echoes: "… those who live in accordance with the Spirit have their minds set on what the Spirit desires."

The star led the Magi to Christ. The Spirit now leads us into Christlikeness.

Carol rephrased to let it percolate. *No*

judgment against us if we have Jesus and the Holy Spirit. Just like the star helped the Wise Men find the Christ Child, having God's Spirit within us helps us know what God wants and live in right relationship with Him.

STAR'S LIGHT AS SPIRITUAL ENLIGHTENMENT

In John 8:12, Jesus declared: "I am the Light of the World. Whoever follows me will never walk in darkness."

Light brings clarity where darkness hid confusion. But just as many missed the star, many missed the Savior right in their midst. Knowledge of the law didn't guarantee recognition of Christ. We can celebrate Christmas and miss Jesus. God won't barge in where He isn't invited.

Carol considered, *God is a gentleman. He doesn't barge in but waits for us to open the door. But choosing to walk around without Him is a little like me looking for a glass of water in the dark and tripping over the tree. You can't see where to walk without light. Jesus, show me the dark corners of my life where you want to shine your light.*

She glanced at the wall in their living room. Above a framed painting of a foggy fishing harbor, a verse: "I am the Light of the World; Whoever follows me shall not walk in darkness. John 8:12."

I almost forgot that was there. Maybe it's a little like Christmas. Too familiar and we just don't notice it anymore—at least not what our culture isn't shoving in front of us.

WE BECOME THE LIGHT OF THE WORLD

Here's the twist in the story: Jesus didn't keep the title "Light of the World" for Himself. In Matthew 5:14-15 He gave it to us: "You are the light of the world… A city on a hill cannot be hidden."

While He walked on earth, He bore the light. Now, as His followers, we carry it. We are called to shine — not to hide. Unless we live in a way that reflects Christ's light, those around us remain in darkness.

Like the star over Bethlehem, we are meant to

guide others to Him.

Think of all Jesus could have accomplished in a long life, but he was crucified at only thirty-three years of age. It's sobering, Lord, to think that you passed the torch to humanity. Down lines of generations and even to me. It's humbling, Lord, and I don't feel worthy or ready, but I want to carry it well."

It was getting late, but tomorrow she had to return to the office. She wanted to finish the chapter. Carol brewed a cup of calming tea and returned to the book.

WE THREE KINGS: KING, GOD, AND SACRIFICE

The familiar carol We Three Kings includes the line: "King and God and Sacrifice." These simple words carry astonishing weight.

- King — Jesus is the promised King of the Jews, yet also the eternal King of Kings.
- God — He is not only sent from God but God Himself, wrapped in human flesh.

- Sacrifice — Despite being King and God, His mission was to lay down His life as the perfect offering to reconcile God and mankind.

This single lyric sums up Christmas: the baby in the manger was King, God, and Sacrifice—salvation His free gift. To try to earn it would insult His suffering. But we can respond with gratitude — and with our own sacrifices, not as payment, but as love offerings.

DOES JESUS GET A CHRISTMAS LIST (OR A BIRTHDAY LIST)?

At Christmas, we exchange gifts with the people we love. But have you ever asked God for His Christmas list? What would be on Jesus' Christmas list that He wanted especially as a gift from you? If you examined your life, what gift could you offer Him this season that would bring Him joy?

Carol prickled. *I'm running at max volunteering at the church. Shouldn't it be obvious? Isn't that the gift?*

Something deep in her Spirit pushed back, forcing deeper questions.

What part of being up front singing is my ego instead of authentic worship? What part of volunteering is social or habit. What part is meeting some expectation or trying to earn a "good girl" from God? Are those really the gifts you want, God? They seem like good ones, but if you need me to surrender even those things so I'm not trying to earn your favor instead of responding in gratitude and love, I will.

The sobering thought needed a moment to sink in before she could read on.

CHRISTMAS LIST FOR GOD

I once dared to ask God for something personal as a Christmas gift — not a possession, but a healing and an assurance. It felt almost greedy, after all He has given. But our Father delights in giving good gifts. And that Christmas, He answered in a way

```
that left no doubt it was from
Him.
        This season, don't just
ask what you can give God. Ask
also: what do you long for Him
to give you? Scripture tells us
God answers prayers that rise
from humble hearts, prayers
aligned with His will, prayers
that bring Him glory.
        Could  your  Christmas
prayer  request  fit  that
description?
```

Gift wrap sat in the guest bedroom, waiting for presents yet to be bought. The family had drawn names for a gift exchange. Carol drew her dad and brother-in-law, both notoriously difficult to buy for. She'd found something and just hoped it would land, recalling the time her husband purchased a new vacuum for her Christmas gift. Newlywed mistake. But Jesus?

What kind of a Christmas gift do you want this year, Jesus? What can I bring to a Heavenly King? One who already gave us all the perfect gift in the form of a baby wrapped in swaddling clothes? Help me listen for Your Christmas list. It'll probably look a little like the misshapen clay pot I made for my dad when I was in kindergarten. Not quite perfectly made, but the effort evident—cherished anyway. Just let me know soon. Christmas is almost here.

PRAYER CHALLENGE

This week, spend time asking God both what He desires from you and what He desires for you. Offer Him a gift of surrender, obedience, or gratitude as your "Christmas present." And then humbly bring your own heart's request to Him, aligning it with His will and glory.

Also reflect on the light you carry. Pray: "Lord, show me where I'm hiding my light. Teach me to shine brightly in my family, my workplace, and my community."

RESPONSE QUESTIONS

1.   King, God, Sacrifice — Which of these three titles means the most to you this Christmas, and why?

2.   What would be on God's "Christmas list" from your life right now? What gift of obedience or surrender could you offer Him this season?

3.   Have you ever asked God for something as a personal "Christmas gift"? How did He answer? Did you ask for something that aligned with His will, which represents His best intentions for You?

4.   Jesus is the Light of the World — but He also calls you the light of the world. What does it

look like in practical terms for your life to shine as a guide to others?

CH 7
HEROD AND THE GREAT PICKLE

Worked hummed along maddeningly. *Why is it like there's a full moon at lawyers' offices in December?* Carol arrived home nearly every day with barely enough energy to cook an acceptable dinner. The stack of low-heeled pumps in the corner and blazers stacked on the sofa attested to the pressure of the grind.

But tomorrow was blocked. The Cookie Exchange night. Billables set aside. Apron firmly tied. Recipes in hand. Five dozen Snickerdoodle cookies produced like clockwork and placed on a red and green holly platter. All in time to brush the flour out of her hair and grab a shower before time to leave.

* * * * * *

Carol walked into the party. The usual suspects, all in Christmas chic. Toned arms and flat bellies. She sucked in momentarily then succumbed to the reality she couldn't hold it all evening. Small talk and smiles. Eventually, the call to walk around the table, filling the large, pink bakery boxes that had been supplied with an assortment of cookies. Carol dutifully complied. Stomach growling at the scent of cinnamon and butter fat, she started to take a treat to eat and then thought the better of it.

Who made this one? Would the others notice that what they brought wasn't the one I chose? Could cookie eating be socially incorrect? She put the cookie dutifully in the box instead of her mouth.

Before she left, Sissy cornered her in the kitchen. "Glad you came." A big hug followed.

Cynicism aside, it felt like Christmas; warped tradition, but part of the warp and weft interweaving the holidays in her family.

Back home, Carol found a pair of stretchy pants, comfy pajamas, and cracked open the lid of the pink box. Brewing a cup of calming tea, she perused the selections carefully and set three cookies on a plate. Biting into the first, she tucked back into her Christmas devotional.

CHAPTER 7 - HEROD AND THE MAGI

WHO WERE THE MAGI?

As we close our pre-Nativity weeks, we turn to the Magi and to Herod. We often call them "wise men," but

Scripture's word is Magi—learned counselors from the East. Their tradition included close observation of the heavens, but they weren't occult magicians. God used a visible sign in the sky to draw seeking hearts to the true King.

The Bible warns against trying to divine the future (what we call astrology today), yet it also shows that creation declares God's glory and that He can employ the heavens to point to His purposes. The Magi followed the light they had—and God gave them more.

Where did their messianic expectation come from? It was likely from the Jewish Scriptures carried into the East during the exile. In Babylon and Persia, figures like Daniel would have shared prophecies such as Numbers 24:17 ("a Star shall come out of Jacob; a scepter shall rise out of Israel") and Daniel's timeline of the coming Anointed One. Over centuries, those prophecies lingered in learned circles across the Parthian/Persian world. So, when an extraordinary sign appeared, the Magi set out—on only partial information, with wholehearted obedience.

What a textured tale. Pagans by any measure, trying to figure out the future and mysteries.

Their culture called them wise men. But their studies made Carol think of her high school friends that pored over their horoscopes in the back of fashion magazines.

Except God let them see something extraordinary. Lord, Your plans seem mysterious but You were weaving this story thousands of years before the event. Allowed the Hebrews to be enslaved by the Babylonians so hints of Your arrival would reach distant lands. Took these men—regarded as wise in their world—back to their people, quietly pre-seeding the gospel's later spread.

Carol stared at the page. What did it say? Wholehearted obedience. *Did they even understand the significance? We have the whole of Scripture and the complete Divine Plan, and we still struggle with obedience. Lord, when you give me a signal, help me to respond with wholehearted obedience, even if it's a long journey to a destination to the unfamiliar.*

She turned another page.

WHO WAS HEROD?

Israel was under Rome. Herod the Great was installed as "king of the Jews" by Roman authority—politically shrewd, ethnically not a Jew, and ferociously insecure. He built cities and temples, but he also executed rivals, even members of his own family. Power without peace made him dangerous.

THE MASSACRE OF THE INNOCENTS

Arriving first in Jerusalem, the Magi assumed a royal birth would be celebrated in the capital. Herod, alarmed, consulted the chief priests and scribes, who cited Micah 5:2: the ruler would come from Bethlehem. Herod then met privately with the Magi, feigning worship and asking them to report back.

But God intervened. After the Magi found the Christ-child and worshiped Him, they were warned in a dream to return by another route. Joseph, likewise warned, fled with Mary and Jesus to Egypt. Herod, thwarted, ordered the slaughter of the boys two and under—a brutal attempt to erase a rival king. Yet God preserved His Son. The Magi's obedience and the provision they brought became part of that protection.

Takeaway: God can bend even hostile powers to advance His purposes; He guides seekers, exposes deceivers, and preserves His promises.

As Carol polished off the last cookie on her plate, she tried to dissect Herod. She shook her head. *How can you understand a madman? But power alone wasn't Herod's core, was it? A power-hungry madman but insecure. When he could have celebrated the miracle, he was too worried about protecting his territory to see the truth. How many people have I met like that in the courtroom?*

Carol finished her tea and put up her mug and plate still pondering Herod.

What do I think of as my territory that needs protection? Herod built walls around his power. I isolate with my business. Lord, are my guardrails ever something that runs contrary to Your intentions? If I trust that You've always got control of Your plans for me, even when it feels like darkness is winning, can I hold my need for control in open hands. When it comes to you, try not to grab the steering wheel out of fear?

PRAYER CHALLENGE

This week, ask God for discernment like the Magi and courage against the spirit of Herod. Pray:

- "Lord, teach me to move on the light I have, and to recognize Your warnings when they come."
- "Guard my heart from fear, envy, or control—the seeds of a Herod spirit. Make me quick to worship, quick to obey."
- "Bless those who are in dark or dangerous seasons. Be their star, their protection, their provision."

Dedicate your chosen Christmas verse to the Lord. Invite Him to weave it through conversations, decisions, and moments of interruption this season.

RESPONSE QUESTIONS

1. Partial light, full obedience. The Magi traveled far with incomplete information. Where might God be asking you to take a faithful step before you have every answer?

2. Guidance and warning. How do you usually sense God's guidance—Scripture, prayer, godly counsel, sanctified common sense? What practice could you strengthen to be more alert to His

"different route" warnings?

    3.   Protection and provision. Where have you seen God quietly arrange timing, resources, or redirection (like with the Magi and Joseph)? How does remembering that story change how you face today's uncertainties?

    4.   Your theme verse. Which verse will you carry through this Christmas, and why does it speak to your current season? What simple rhythm (lock-screen, sticky note, morning prayer) will keep it in view?

CH. 8
THE TOWER OF THE FLOCK

When Carol pulled into the driveway the next day, the postal worker was just about to load the mail into the box. Instead, as Carol slowed the car to open the garage door, he waved and smiled, heading over. Same guy for the last several years. Carol lowered the car window and accepted the personal delivery. Another stack of Christmas guilt cards.

As she entered the house, Grant was already home. She handed the stack of mail to him.

"These all mine?"

She grimaced. "You can have them!" She remembered last year. She'd done the whole Christmas letter with updates about the family through the year. Spent hours finding the perfect pictures of all the family members, organized into an artistic collage. They had been ordered and arrived well before Christmas. Grant promised to address them. And then they sat. She discovered them again in July. He'd just laughed and said they should send them out as a half-Christmas update. It still annoyed her.

Grant tore open the first card on top and burst into laughter. "Carol, you gotta see this. A picture of Kent across the street, collapsed on the floor under a fully decorated Christmas tree. Wonder if it was staged or Lisa just caught a handyman fail?"

Taking the card, Carol had to admit it was pretty comical. Better than some picture-perfect Christmas nonsense that read like a carefully curated social media page.

This next week was Christmas, and Carol had almost gotten to the far side of fake-it-till-you-make-it. After dinner, she sat quietly admiring the tree lights illuminating the ceiling. Rain gently pattered on the roof. Grant had built a cheery fire. It was beginning to feel a lot like Christmas. She pulled out her devotional.

CHAPTER 8: THE CAMEL, THE SHEEP & NO ROOM AT THE INN

Up to now, we've studied the gifts and journeys that prepared for Christ's arrival. Now we turn to the moment of His birth. Many of us feel we know this story inside and out—through Luke's Gospel, nativity sets, Sunday school plays, and Christmas readings. But cultural retellings have added layers of myth that sometimes blur the richness of the actual story.

Just as the scribes of Jesus' day read Scripture so often that they missed the Messiah standing before them, we can miss details bursting with meaning if we skim too quickly. God orchestrated Jesus' arrival with precision—down to the very setting of His birth.

NO ROOM AT THE INN

We often picture Mary and Joseph turned away by an innkeeper, forced into a barn. But the Greek word "kataluma" can also mean guest room. In traditional Bethlehem homes, the upper room was for guests, while the lower room was shared space—sometimes even housing prized animals overnight.

Hospitality and family were both big concepts in Biblical times. The Bible tells us that Mary and Joseph traveled to Bethlehem because a census had been ordered that required them to travel to their ancestral home to be counted. Mary and Joseph's relatives were from Bethlehem. Their residency stemmed back to the time of the Book of Ruth where Mary's relative Boaz took in the widow Ruth who would be one of a few women graced with inclusion in Jesus' genealogy.

At the time Mary and Joseph arrived, it was also likely just before the Passover celebration in Jerusalem, just five miles away. With Passover approaching in nearby Jerusalem, the "little town" was overflowing—crammed to the top with guests. If there had been such a thing as hotels, perhaps they would have indeed had a "no vacancy" sign due to this influx of travelers, but that is not an accurate picture of where Mary and Joseph would have stayed. It's almost certain they would have stayed with family.

Our retellings make it sound as if Mary barely got into town, hopped off a donkey and immediately went into labor, tired from the journey. More accurately, they were there for a short time before Mary went into labor. While family had taken them in because hospitality was a requirement and a tremendous honor in the ancient biblical world, now there was likely a practical problem. The guests in the house were there to participate in the Passover. They couldn't do so if they were unclean. Under Levitical law, the issue of blood with Mary's labor would make her unclean and everyone in the household disqualified along with her.

Carol was reminded of Christmas' when she

and Grant were in the early days of their marriage, when Grant's parents were still alive.

Ha!—Mary and Joseph had to travel to visit their relatives for Christmas, too. They were supposed to travel one day to see Grant's family in the Bay Area. The next day, her parents would host their Christmas dinner. Sissy was already married and, for no discernable reason except maybe to say she was hosting, she insisted on an open house the day after Christmas. Living in an apartment then, Grant and Carol lacked room to play host. The different families would never have consolidated their Christmases anyway. Especially the Christmas after the twins were born, the travel and overload nearly squished the joy out of the holidays. Maybe that was it. Overflowing Christmas hospitality but no room for grace.

Carol grimaced. *At least I wasn't going to deliver a baby at home and have everyone grossing out about the details.*

The practicality hit. *It wasn't that they didn't have a place to stay, they were just unwelcome. No room wasn't about the proverbial Inn, it was about human hearts. Mary's due date was spoiling the party. At her most vulnerable, Mary was being whispered about in the kitchen and labeled a big problem. The families were intending to worship God, but their desire to put their celebration in front of Mary's vulnerability meant they missed the very arrival of God on earth.*

She couldn't put the book down at the cliffhanger. What were they going to do with Mary? Carol slowed, reading with deliberation as a map she'd never seen before unfolded before her.

THE SHEPHERDS AND THEIR LEVITICAL SHEEP

Meanwhile, shepherds were "abiding in the fields at night." That detail matters. Ordinary flocks were kept farther from town. But Bethlehem's sheep were Levitical flocks, raised specifically for sacrifice in Jerusalem.

Because these sheep were intended to be sacrificed, there were special requirements placed on the sheep and their shepherds. In order to be an acceptable sacrifice, the sheep had to be kept outside for 365 days, and this is why the Christmas Story tells us specifically that these shepherds were tending their flocks outside in the fields at night. Other shepherds might have other options, but this was a requirement for the Levitical flock. To be an acceptable sacrifice, the sheep had to be perfect

To best keep these Levitical lambs from potential harm, the shepherds of Bethlehem would take the ewes to a birthing cave when it came close to their time to deliver. This cave near Bethlehem was known as the Tower of the Flock. Inside were limestone mangers or feeding troughs. The shepherds would keep this cave extremely clean because it was a maternity ward for the sheep. As the newborn lambs arrived, the shepherds would place each lamb into a limestone manger to wrap the lamb in strips of swaddling cloth meant to protect them and keep them blemish-free.

Carol's eyes were drawn from the page to the

nativity set sitting on the antique buffet. *Like the wise men, every nativity set I've ever seen makes it seem like the wise men and shepherds all arrived in unison at some barn out back. But I've never clearly heard how the shepherds got there or why shepherds at all. I never knew they were responsible for preparing the sacrificial lambs.*

The foreshadowing rifled over Carol's soul like a dark storm cloud, making her shiver. Reading the next words, she froze.

> There isn't a lot of information about Jesus' birth in the Bible so we cannot verify the accuracy of what I'm about to contend next and I want to make that very clear; however, the information we do have and the information we have from history and customs makes a very interesting scenario a very real possibility.

What were the words foreshadowing? How does it lead from Levitical shepherds to a delivery room scene?

THE TOWER OF THE FLOCK

Imagine the timing. As Mary's time grew near and the entire household risked being unclean and disqualified from participating in the Passover if she gave birth in the house, there may have been good reason to try to find somewhere else for Mary to deliver her baby, particularly somewhere that would afford Mary some privacy. This special birthing cave used by the Levitical shepherds appears to have been located on land that would have traditionally been owned by Boaz, Mary's relative. The family may have continued to have some ownership rights. It was not lambing season when Mary and Joseph arrived so the cave would have been unoccupied and ritually clean. It would not be unthinkable that they moved Mary to the Tower of the Flock as she went into labor.

Luke 2:7 tells us, "She brought forth her firstborn

```
son,    and    wrapped   him    in
swaddling  clothes,   and   laid
him  in  a  manger;  because  there
was   no   room   for   them   in   the
inn."
```

No, no, it was a barn. A warm barn out back of the house with clean straw and the cattle lowing while the baby slept!

Reading the words slowing again, the gentle childhood manger scene ripped in two, replaced by a feeling as cold and hard as a picture of a stone manger. Carol's heart rendered a soft cry.

God, this imagery is almost too much. Your tiny body brought into this world in the same place as the lambs destined for sin sacrifice. Laid down on the limestone mangers used during the breeding season to protect the lambs from imperfections that would disqualify them from being brutally cut short. Wrapped in swaddling clothes intended for unexpected burial. And Your hand still in such incredible detail. This place reserved on family lands owned back to the time of Ruth and Boaz, a Redeemer kinsman story.

Carol's heart broke with the kind of breaking that leads straight to God's heart and to a renewal of faith and relationship. She continued reading through misty eyes.

We're told in the Christmas Story that angels appeared to the shepherds with good news and the shepherds went to find the baby. We're told that Jesus' first visitors were not the Kings from the East but the lowly shepherds. They would have been dirty and smelly from living outside with the sheep. More interesting, because of their occupation, they were unclean and unable to participate in the very Passover celebration they made possible. They were unclean and unafraid to be in the presence of a woman ritually unclean because of her recent labor and delivery.

Carol pictured the odd scene. Her brows knit. *How unfair to Mary. Strangers? Shepherds? Invited to invade divine maternity room? How did the shepherds know? Did they hear the baby cry? What would Mary have thought when they walked in? Afraid she would be unwelcome in yet another place?*

HOW DID THE SHEPHERDS KNOW?

Angels told them. Why? They were not just any shepherds. There may have been no other group of people that would have understood the symbolic meanings behind where and how this special baby was born except these Levitical shepherds.

These shepherds were in charge of raising the sheep for the sacrifice to remove sins but because of their dirty, smelly job, they were unclean and unable to participate. But the angels invite them to be the first to meet Jesus. The ones excluded from the table of sacrifice were welcomed to the witness the newborn true Sacrifice.

Well, wasn't that just like God? Honoring the women myrrh bearers that society disregarded as lesser than? Now he's taking the people who never thought they could participate in the means to remove their sins because they were being used as

the set up crew and elevating them to first witnesses.
But wait. Those shepherds just finished packing up
the baby lambs for slaughter and ritually cleaning
the birthing cave. What would they have thought
about a baby wrapped in swaddling and placed in the
stone feeding manger?

The angels told them they would find the baby in "the" manger—not just any manger. Wouldn't these shepherds have thought of the Tower? It was where tradition said the Messiah would be born. It was where the sacrificial lambs were born. The angels invited them to see the Lamb of God swaddled just as their lambs had been.

I wonder if they knew that this baby, like their Levitical lambs, was not born to be an earthly king, but born to die for sin? And these shepherds were charged above all things to never leave the watch over their Levitical flocks and yet they abandoned them to find this baby.

```
    Symbolically there was no
further    need    for    these
Levitical   sacrificial   sheep
because   the   Lamb   of   God   had
arrived to take away the sins
of the world.
```

Again—the unconventional characters of the nativity, wise men and shepherds, leaving everything to find Jesus. Well, I guess an angel would convince me to abandon a court hearing to find Jesus. Right?

Grant's television show was ending. He leaned over and looked at Carol closely. "What were you reading? You look all teared up. One of those heart-jerker romance novels?"

Carol debated trying to explain, but there was too much detail, and she still felt raw. She'd explain another time. She smiled weakly. "Yeah. The best kind of love story."

PRAYER CHALLENGE

This week, ask God to strip away the "cultural varnish" so you can see Jesus' birth with fresh wonder. Thank Him for the precision of His plan—that even the manger, the swaddling cloths, and the shepherds shouted His purpose.

Pray: "Lord, help me not miss Your details. Teach me to see where You are already at work, weaving meaning into places I overlook. And help me welcome You into every corner of my life, even the ones that feel unclean."

RESPONSE QUESTIONS

1.   We often picture Mary and Joseph in a barn—but Scripture hints at something richer. How does it change your perspective to see Jesus' birth tied to sacrifice from the very first moment?

2.   The shepherds abandoned their flocks to seek Jesus. What "flocks" (responsibilities, routines, distractions) might you need to set aside temporarily in order to focus on Christ this season?

3.   How does knowing the detail in Jesus' arrival change your perspective on Christmas as a celebration of His birth?

CH 9
OUR PLANS, HIS PURPOSES

Christmas week arrived, ready or not. Despite a few blocked days before the event, Carol's preparations weren't nearly complete. The house still couldn't be called guest-ready. Grant and the kids seemed to be enjoying things just as they were, watching nostalgic Christmas movies and leaving snack plates randomly stacked around the house. Carol debated the phrase, "If you can't beat 'em, join 'em" while sporadically pivoting between just that and furiously trying to make clean spots, asking herself, *When is it good enough?*

After a cleaning bout, she sat down for a well-deserved break, trying to shake off the resentment. She seemed to be the only one who cared about the things that were keeping her anything but relaxed. A good time for a heart check. She picked up the devotional, hoping to find some peace between its covers.

CHAPTER 9: MARY, JOSEPH &
THE ANGELS

THE COST OF BEING MARY —
TEEN MOM

When we think of Mary,
it's easy to put her on a
pedestal — the "Holy Mother,"
somehow set apart from
ordinary life. But in reality,
she was a young girl, likely no
more than fifteen. In today's
terms, we might compare her to
a "teen mom." Yet it was
precisely her humility,
availability, and willingness
to obey that drew God's favor.

Mary's "yes" to God came
at great cost. No one had ever
experienced such a divine
pregnancy before, and it was
unreasonable to expect others
would believe her story. She
risked her reputation, her
engagement, her future dreams.
To be God's servant meant
surrendering everything.

Carol reflected, *I guess I'm not the only one*

finding it hard to be a mother. Mary was so young to be a mom or to carry such a heavy emotional weight. God trusted her with the burden to process His plans when it risked everything for her. Being a servant to my family is costing me this week. Bu, I guess if Jesus could wash the feet of the disciples, I can wash a few dirty dishes without getting my self-entitlement involved. Anyway, why am I doing this to myself at Christmas? All the self-imposed expectations. Mamas work hard to make Christmas happen, but when the picture overshadows the family's actual needs, maybe it's time for me to step back and find my fuzzy slippers instead of a mop.

ELIZABETH: GOD'S GIFT OF ENCOURAGEMENT

God did not leave Mary alone. Her cousin Elizabeth, much older and unexpectedly pregnant with John the Baptist, became her ally and mentor. Luke 1 records Gabriel's announcement to Mary, her acceptance, and then her haste to visit Elizabeth in the Judean hill country.

This wasn't a short stroll. Depending on the town, Mary traveled 80-100 miles, likely in a caravan, over several days. Why the rush? Scripture says she "hurried" — a word that suggests eagerness, even urgency. She longed to see the sign Gabriel had given: Elizabeth, once barren, now visibly six months along.

When Mary arrived, Elizabeth's baby leapt in the womb, and Elizabeth, filled with the Spirit, cried out: "Blessed are you among women, and blessed is the child you will bear! … Blessed is she who has believed that the Lord would fulfill His promises to her!" (Luke 1:42, 45).

Elizabeth's words were confirmation, comfort, and counsel. For three months Mary stayed, helping Elizabeth and preparing herself. God provided a mentoring relationship at just the moment Mary needed it most.

All this talk about babies and close

relationships had Carol's mind floating back to her conversation with Liz. She thought of how she'd baked an extra batch of Snickerdoodle cookies last night—Granny's famous family recipe of lore (also suspiciously like the version in the 1950's Betty Crocker Cookbook).

She turned toward Grant. "Hey, honey, I'm going to pop over to see Liz and her family if you guys are good until lunchtime."

He shot her a raised-eyebrow, quizzical look. "Something up?"

She quickly glanced at the kids, seemingly engrossed in the movie. "Tell you later. I just know she needs a friend right now, and Granny's Snickerdoodles are the closest thing I have to medicine and love. I'm going to bring them a plate."

He nodded. "We'll still be here when you get back."

At the mention of Snickerdoodles, Marcus suddenly came out of his TV trance. "Not all the cookies Mom. They're my favorites."

Carol grinned, "There's more in the kitchen and you've got 'ins' with the bakery." Yup, they'd all be right where she left them. Maybe not a perfect Christmas card picture, but the best one this year had been Kent and Lisa's topped tree. Real life.

* * * * *

A few hours later, after a heartfelt visit with Liz, Carol returned, heart brimming with gratitude for the children she'd been able to carry successfully, now still sitting in rumpled pajamas, annoying one another, and spreading cookies crumbs so the vacuum wouldn't starve. Carol reopened the journal, hoping to finish before Christmas.

MARY TREASURED AND PONDERED

Later, after Jesus' birth and the shepherds' visit, Luke tells us: "Mary treasured up all these things and pondered them in her heart" (Luke 2:19). This is one of my favorite Bible verses!

The Greek words carry rich meaning: "treasured" implies carefully storing and safeguarding memories; "pondered" suggests connecting the dots, reflecting until understanding comes. Mary models how we should respond when God's plan is bigger than we can grasp. Treasure the moment. Ponder patiently. Wait for the pieces to fall into place.

Carol reflected on everything she'd read the past few weeks. All that had transpired. *I want to create memories to treasure. Not just the hustle and bustle of the office or even the holiday, but the moments where we connect—with family, with God. And, what a great idea to keep the memories of the challenges and answers to "connect dots" to better see God's plan. Maybe my New Year's goal will be keeping a Faith Journal. If I can memorialize the jewels—the moments that God answers my prayers or reveals Himself in special ways—maybe those can be a place to strengthen my faith when the storms come.*

JOSEPH: THE QUIET STRENGTH

Joseph is often the most overlooked figure in the nativity, yet his role is profound. Engagement in that culture was binding — to break it required divorce. When Mary was found pregnant, Joseph faced a dilemma: expose her publicly, or end things quietly. His instinct was mercy.

Then God intervened. An angel told him in a dream that

Mary's child was from the Holy Spirit. Notice: the angel didn't command Joseph to marry her — he simply removed Joseph's fear that she was unfaithful. Joseph still had to choose obedience.

And he did. He accepted shame, misunderstanding, and difficulty, embracing Mary and adopting Jesus as his son. That earthly adoption mirrors our heavenly adoption: just as Joseph brought Jesus fully into his family, God brings us fully into His through Christ.

1st John 4:18 came to Carol's mind: "There is no fear in love…"

So why was Joseph afraid? He wasn't the one facing shame and death—that was Mary. His fear was that she had been unfaithful, didn't love him enough to wait for him. And he considered this carefully and couldn't see any human way to explain away the pregnancy, so his trust in their love fractured. But, before it could completely break, God. Echoes of Eden, in Eve's fear that God was withholding something good, fracturing trust in his His love. And God intervening through adopting us as true sons and daughters despite everything the Accuser has to say about us.

And it seems that Joseph and Mary didn't have such a simple start to their marriage. The difficulties didn't go away. Their intimacy plans put on hold. Ordered to travel at a most inconvenient time. Traveling in the same car long distance is bad enough. I can't imagine how cranky I would have been if I was a pregnant Mary getting bounced on a camel all that way. There could have been words. Some are-we-there-yet moments. And after settling into a new home for just a couple of years, they had to flee to a completely foreign land because of a threat to the life of the baby. That couldn't have been easy. When Joseph signed up for obedience, he couldn't have had any idea!

Carol looked over at Grant. They'd been together more than half their lifetimes now. Knew all the dirt on each other. Had a near lifetime of memories that, like strands in a rope, intertwined into something more than their parts and could hold things together. There had been challenges, like any long-term marriage. Fight Rules had been negotiated. Grace Rules included.

Carol put down her book. Tonight, she would pray for her sons' future wives. Now, it was time to make dinner.

* * * * * *

That night, the family walked Holiday

Village Drive. A local tradition, the two-mile-long drive was seasonally blocked off to through traffic. All the homeowners went all-out with creative Christmas yard displays. The Holly Trolley took visitors from the parking lot, where disposable cups of hot chocolate with marshmallows were available for purchase. With gloved hands, watching their breath blow clouds into the night air, the family set off. It never disappointed. They neared the end of the walk tired but joyful.

Back home, Carol threw on a Christmas apron, mostly for show and attitude, and started work on the pumpkin-gingerbread cheesecake she'd promised to take to tomorrow's family dinner. When she'd volunteered to bring a dessert, her mother had replied, "Well, I guess we could always use *another* pie." Self-sufficiency that hardly allowed for anyone else's participation. Carol tried to set her feelings about the remark aside.

Maybe like Jesus felt about that church that wanted to print its own money. But I knew deep inside, Mom will appreciate my effort. I hope it makes her feel seen to have someone else at least try to bear some of the workload.

There will be that terrible Tamale Pie. Not even a Christmas dish. I wonder if it evolved from a recipe that may have once been edible? Now, it's mostly warm cornmeal with some bits of hamburger and random olives. I loathe it, but somehow once

Mom got it in her head it was my favorite nothing I've said has got that notion unstuck— just one of those weird traditions now. Always made. Never eaten. Never omitted. But those are the idiosyncrasies that make family memories we'll talk about after Mom is gone.

Pie baked. Apron off. Feet talking, and not nicely. Carol was ready for a Christmas tea and a final dose of devotional before the big family day tomorrow.

ANGELS: MESSENGERS AND WARRIORS

The angels of Luke 2 may be the most iconic nativity figures. At first, one angel appeared to the shepherds: "Do not be afraid. I bring you good news that will cause great joy for all the people." Then suddenly, the sky was filled with a great company of the heavenly host, praising God.

Their message had two parts: Glory to God -and- Joy to people.

But notice: Jesus Himself was not born into joy. He was born to die. Hebrews 12:2 says:

"For the joy set before Him He endured the cross." His earthly mission was marked by pain, but future joy motivated Him — the joy of saving us, of fulfilling His Father's plan.

The shepherds' fear was overwhelming — the Greek says they were "mega phobeo phobos," terrified out of their wits. No wonder: the sky blazed with God's glory, brighter than sun and stars, and the angels' chorus thundered across the fields. It was as if heaven itself had crowded into earth's night sky.

It's almost comical imagining that scene with the night sky suddenly brighter than the day. Maybe what the dog feels like on the Fourth of July? No, that's too irreverent. Still, I hope there was some time before that first angel and the heavenly hosts. Other biblical appearances of a single angel caused men to fall on their faces in fear. What would all the hosts of heavenly angels be like? And those angels must have been so overwhelmed themselves to see God's plan for mankind. Joy outside the birthing cave in the fields of the shepherds. Inside, all the symbols of a baby fated to death.

> I wonder, too, if those
> angels came not only to
> celebrate but also to guard.
> Scripture shows us Satan's
> repeated attempts to derail
> God's plan — including Herod's
> massacre. That night, heaven's
> armies stood as witnesses and
> warriors at the manger. God
> always protects His plan.
> Angels attended Jesus' birth.
> Magi made it possible to escape
> to Egypt. At every turn, God
> was ahead of Satan's attempts
> to prematurely end Jesus' life
> and ministry.

We always make it pretty—a heavenly choir. More like legions of heavenly warriors ready to do battle! What a picture.

Carol turned the last page and shut the book.

Lord, I think I'm ready to celebrate your arrival now. Ready to surrender my plans knowing how incredible and intricate Your plans are. Ready to give a little more grace and space for people in the middle of my rainbow world. And, even in the middle of that, to keep my eyes and ears open in case You have something for me as I'm doing other things.

PRAYER CHALLENGE

This week, ask God to give you:

- Mary's humility — a willingness to surrender your future to His plan.
- Joseph's obedience — courage to step into misunderstood, costly faithfulness.
- The angels' joy — eyes to see the glory of God's plans and rejoice even in hardship.

Pray also for discernment to treasure what God is doing in your life, even when you don't yet understand it. Wait for the dots to connect.

RESPONSE QUESTIONS

1. Mary and Joesph said yes though it cost her reputation and dreams. Where might obedience to God cost you right now?

2. Luke 2:19:"But Mary treasured up all these things and pondered them in her heart." Mary didn't try to explain everything, fix everything, or even understand everything. Mary treasured and pondered rather than rushing to explain. What do you need to reflect on, sit with, and ponder, instead of demanding quick answers?

3. The angels rejoiced, though Jesus was born to die, because they saw the miracle for mankind in God's plans. How does remembering

"the joy set before Him" strengthen you in present trials? How does the story help you remember God is in control?

CH. 10
THE ARRIVAL

Carol and her family arrived at Mom's House (somehow always known as Mom's House even if Dad lived there too) right on time. Carol had won the argument—the boys hadn't worn sweats. Clarissa had almost made them late by taking an hour to herself in the shared kids' bathroom. Carol had almost forgotten the pumpkin-gingerbread cheesecake in the refrigerator. The arrival wasn't neat or orderly, but it was timely.

Gifts were exchanged. Some likes, a few misses. Sissy fussed in the kitchen. Carol tried to stay out of the way. Dad made a huge fire that nearly roasted everyone out of the house despite the winter weather outside. Grant's brother cracked a slightly inappropriate joke. The men collapsed, vying for the reclining seats—a group post-turkey tryptophan nap.

* * * * * *

When recovered enough for more overindulgence, they waddled back to the big table for desserts. Carol suggested, "Why don't we read the Christmas story from Luke?"

A groan from Grant's brother. A look from Marcus of…embarrassment?

Sissy replied, "Same one we just heard at church, right? Same every year?"

The room felt smaller. Everyone was looking at her expectantly. Impatiently. Marcus and Michael with dessert plates already in hand. Carol ducked her head. "Maybe not quite. I've been revisiting it the last few weeks. There's some stuff in there I really needed to be reminded of."

Grant looked quizzical. "I know you've been pretty into that book on your side table this week. Like what?"

Carol smiled uncertainly. What to share? What was too much? And why was everyone so reluctant to talk about Christmas…on Christmas? Or were they all talking about the same thing when the holiday was mentioned?

Clarissa nudged Carol's elbow. "Go ahead, Mom. You started the conversation. What did you mean?"

What am I so afraid of?

"I guess simply that Christmas is supposed to celebrate Jesus' arrival—his birthday. But Jesus at Christmas isn't the host waiting for us to show up so much as a guest we almost forget to invite."

That won a look of approval from Grant.

Sissy shifted uncomfortably. Just as quickly as the moment connected, it was gone as Grant's brother announced, "I'm having some of that cheesecake. Anyone else with me?"

* * * * * *

Back home, everyone else crashed from a sugar overload, Grant and Carol sat, watching the dying embers of the Christmas Eve fire. Grant asked, "That book you've been reading must have had a lot to unpack. Want to share your biggest takeaway?"

Carol blinked, surprised. "Oh, there's a lot."

She paused. Thought a moment.

Grant added, "Anything to do with the new pillows? Fall your knees?"

Remembering her own fall on her knees, Carol cracked a slight smile. "Just that every time we fall down—bow down to Christ in love and surrender rather than fear and control—we move back toward Eden's intended intimacy with God we were created to know."

He didn't pursue it further just then, but the look on his face told Carol that he was pondering these things in his heart.

SUMMARY RESPONSE QUESTIONS

Theme: Treasuring the Story Together:

1. Which figure or symbol in the nativity meant the most to you this season — and why?
2. Which gift's symbolism (purity, prayer, provision, friendship, sacrifice) resonated most with you?
3. Was there a moment in these weeks where God surprised you with a new insight? What detail in the nativity story made you say, "Wow, I've never noticed that before"?
4. If you could take one truth from the nativity into this Christmas or maybe even carry it forward into the new year, what would it be? If you had to choose one truth to treasure and ponder going into Christmas, what would it be?
5. Has doing this study shaped the way you see your role in leading others in faith and worship or in the way you may want to volunteer at your church?

Made in United States
North Haven, CT
19 October 2025

80985247R00078